T0197603

Introduction

As a follower of Christ I'd like to share my testimony with children of all ages of how to become a Christian. I was eight years old when I decided that I wanted to be a writer. Before then, I had always wanted to be an artist because my favorite subject was art. But on a drive back from Burger King one night, I felt like someone was talking to my heart. I thought, "Hey, if I was an author I could reach more people for Christ and I could still be an artist, but they would call me a book illustrator." I knew that I could do this in my heart.

At the age of twelve I was baptized publicly so that everyone knew I was a Christian. That is the greatest sense of humility for Christ to be dunked underneath holy water by a preacher in front of at least two hundred strangers. But I was proud because now I would grow up in the image of Christ. I still sin; I'm not perfect but I try to be like Jesus in every way possible. The easiest way to do this is be talking to him daily from your heart and reading the literature he has given to us, the Truth, his Holy Word: the Bible. I prefer King James Version myself, but for recently born-again Christians I believe the New International Version simplifies the words best.

I thought if I could reach at least one person with each shipment of my books sent out to a store, then I would feel better that I actually lived the life God wanted me to, for Him.

In the inside cover and inside back cover I wanted to put the "how to become a Christian" steps. Many people have written thousands of different versions of these steps, but I prefer the Vacation Bible School steps, so called the ABC's of Becoming A Christian.

Three Orphans

Marjorie May Pearson

AuthorHouse™
1663 Liberty Drive
Bloomington, IN 47403
www.authorhouse.com
Phone: 833-262-8899

Because of the dynamic nature of the Internet, any web addresses or links contained in this book may have changed
since publication and may no longer be valid. The views expressed in this work are solely those of the author and do not
necessarily reflect the views of the publisher, and the publisher hereby disclaims any responsibility for them.

Any people depicted in stock imagery provided by Getty Images are models,
and such images are being used for illustrative purposes only.
Certain stock imagery © Getty Images.

This book is printed on acid-free paper.

ISBN: 978-1-4520-3676-2 (sc)

Library of Congress Control Number: 2010915975

Print information available on the last page.

Published by AuthorHouse 08/19/2021

authorHOUSE®

A – Admit that you are a sinner.

B – Believe that Jesus is God's Son. Believe that He came to earth to die on a cross to take away your punishment some 2,000 years ago. Believe that God's gift to you is forgiveness of your sins.

C – Confess your faith in Jesus Christ as Savior and Lord.

Please enjoy this book.
Love your sister in Christ,

Marjorie May Pearson

On the other side of Sunny Brook Stream lived three orphans. Their names were Joanne (Jo for short), Ash, and Bo. On this particular day they were going to snatch some food from a pear tree, but the problem was the tree was too high. So Jo held Bo up, couldn't reach; then she tried holding Ash up, he held Bo up, and Bo shook the first limb he could grab. Yes! They got six pears, two each. Mmm! Juicy!

"Come on, Jo," Ash said, running into the cave with his pears, "let's go in, and read that new book you got from town."

"The Bible?" Jo asked.

"Yea," Bo ran behind Ash inside the cave, dropping pears as he went. Jo picked up each pear Bo had dropped and after handing his pears back, Jo read a chapter from the book of Philippians.

"This comes from chapter four," Jo read. "Verse thirteen says that we can do all things through Christ who strengthens us. All we have to do is pray and Jesus will take care of us, because He is our Savior."

"Jo?" Ash questioned. "Does Jesus take care of us, now that our parents are gone?"

"Yes, and He will take care of each one of us each day or even if we are by ourselves."

"Jo, how did your parents die?" Bo asked, staring at Jo.

"Mine were killed in the war," Ash spoke up. "Dad was a soldier and Ma was a nurse."

"Jo," Bo pleaded.

"Same as yours, Bo, the illness took them. Now let's pray that the illness won't get us; bow your heads," Jo replied closing the Bible, and getting on her knees beside Ash and Bo. Taking their hands they prayed together in silence.

On the other side of the lands lived the robbers named Johnny, Will, Travis, and Davey. They were planning to find the orphans hideout. They only followed the orphans' footprints to the stream, and then gave up. They were determined to find the children to torture and slave them until dusk. Will and Johnny wanted the girl as a maid. Travis and Davey thought the two boys would make good beggars in town.

One day Jo told Ash and Bo to stay at the cave while she went into town to get a newspaper. In the little town, Sunnyshine newspapers were free, so orphan children didn't have to steal them. On her way back she found a little pigeon, she then took the pigeon up from the ground, and tied, with a ribbon from her hair, the newspaper around the pigeon's leg, knowing it was a carrier pigeon; she walked on to the bad guy's hideout.

Jo wanted to see what the bandits were doing. She found out! She got a close up look. The bandits were not home. Jo carefully walked in the cabin. CriPPle CrACK!!

"Who's there?" She said scared.

"Chirp, chirp, chirp," a little bird hopped on the leaves outside on the windowsill.

"You scared me little chirpster," said Jo talking to the little bird.

"Yes! We got the loot, Will," Jo heard Johnny, one of the robbers outside the OPEN door.

"Ssshh! Be quiet, Johnny. Someone is in the house. C'mon," Travis whispered.

"I'll get him if he tries to come out here," Davey told Travis.

"Come on out who ever is in our cabin!" Will shouted.

"Now he'll never come out," Johnny told Will.

"Me and Travis will go in there after them, Johnny," Davey said.

"I'll go in through the back door," Will replied, "Johnny you go under the house."

"Will do, Will," Johnny replied sarcastically.

"What will I do? What will I do?" Jo wondered to herself. "I know, I'll hide in the cabinet."

"Well you were wrong, Travis, no one is in here except that little bird on the sill," Davey said, raising his gun.

BANG!

"That bird's dead," Johnny said coming up out of the trap door from under the house.

Jo took a deep breath, but couldn't help it, "Aahhh-chooo!"

"What was that?" exclaimed Will walking in the back door.

"I have no idea," answered Johnny.

"In the cabinet," Travis said pointing.

"I'll look," said Davey kneeling down behind the couch, into the China cabinet.

"Uh-oh," Jo whispered.

"Ah ha," Davey shouted grabbing Jo's wrist, jerking her out from among the dishes.

"Ouch!" Jo shouted. Davey threw her down in the circle of his brothers. Travis grabbed her back up, by her arm. "Stand, Missy!"

"Let me go," Jo struggled.

"No!"

"Yes," Will and Johnny shouted together.

"Ouch," Jo repeated as Travis slung her back on the floor at Davey's feet.

Back at the cave Ash and Bo were reading the letter from Jo, she had written on the Sunnyshine newspaper. "What does it say?" Bo asked Ash.

"It says," Ash read aloud, " 'I've gone to the BANDIT'S HOUSE!'" Ash exclaimed the last words Jo had written. Ash stood up quickly and ran out of the cave, "come on Bo, we have to run, Jo has been there way too long!"

Bo ran out of the cave, "Are you sure, Ash?"

"Yes, now come on," Ash jerked Bo's arm and started to run.

After they got to Sunny Brook, the stream between their cave and the bandit's cabin, they slowed their pace, and started to hum to keep their courage up.

"Through the trees, through the stream, and through the bushes we go, we are near the bandits' house now. Will they shoot us with their guns?" Ash and Bo looked at each other as they went through the last bushes towards the cabin.

"I hope not," Bo replied talking in a whisper.

"Let me go, murderers," Jo yelled at the four brothers.

"Hey now, Jo, we aren't murderers," Will used his smirk innocence to correct Jo, "We're bandits."

"Why would you think we were murderers?" Johnny questioned.

"Davey knows," Jo pointed in anger. Davey slapped her hand down back to the floor.

"I do?"

"Yes! You killed my friend!" Jo shouted in tears. She started to weep for the bird that had died.

"What friend?" Davey looked curiously down at Jo.

"That bird! Don't act like you don't know," Jo brought her hand back up and pointed angrily at Davey again. Davey slapped Jo hard across the face. Jo cried on the floor in the midst of the four brothers. Will put his hands up on his hips. Johnny grabbed Davey's shoulder and shook his head for Davey not to get violent.

"Keep that hand out of my face, and we'll discuss this without accusations," Davey assured her.

"Stop it, Davey! Just stop!" Will shouted.

"Why?" Davey looked up at Will.

"'Cause he said so," Johnny replied, looking down at Davey firmly.

"Shut up," Davey shouted in Johnny's direction.

"Good idea, Davey," Travis defended Davey.

Jo started to stand up, "You coward!" She looked up at Davey nastily.

"Why I ought to," Davey started to say, before Johnny interrupted him.

"You ought to what?"

"I ought to knock your block off, Johnny! Stop interrupting me!"

Before Jo knew it, Johnny and Davey were arguing right over her. They would shuffle to the right, then to the left, but she was still under them. Then Will took Johnny's side and Travis took Davey's side that caused more fighting. Then slaps were being thrown and Will took hold of Davey's hands, and Travis grabbed Johnny around the waist, then those two turned on Will and Travis for getting into it. Jo scrambled out from under the fighters, and near the window on the other side of the room near the chimney. For a while she just sat there praying to God, about what she was going to do, until they knew that they were really fighting over nothing.

Suddenly Jo heard a soft creak and a whisper, "Jo, psst! Jo." She saw Ash, who was behind the couch, and had come up through the trapdoor on the other side of the den.

"Ash," Jo loudly whispered, but Ash quickly quieted her.

"Come over here," he whispered. Jo crawled as quietly as she could on the creaking floor, even though she didn't think the four boys could really be disturbed. Jo crept down the trapdoor and waited on Ash down under the house on the soft earth.

"I left them a note," Ash said as he gave Jo a partially heavy bag, grabbed her wrist, and ran with her towards where he had left Bo.

The three orphans ran all the way back to the cave with five bags full of silver and gold.

Later that day, after Jo had gotten away, Davey and Johnny were finally separated, and Will had found the note from Ash. He read it aloud in a tempered loud voice, " 'Thanks for the money. See ya later, boys!' Aaah! I'm going to get those orphans!" Will's voice echoed through the surrounding woods. He threw the paper down on the wooden cabin floor.

At the cave the orphans decided to count their newly acquired money. Jo counted, "One hundred, two hundred, three hundred…"

"You know, Jo, Will might be pretty upset that we got his gold," Ash suggested with a smirk.

"You think so?" Jo asked smirking back.

"Yeah, probably," Bo said innocently, not getting the hint of sarcasm Jo and Ash used. Jo and Ash just laughed at their findings. Bo joined in the laughter, even though he didn't know why he was laughing.

At the bandits' cabin Will, Johnny, Davey, and Travis were thinking of a plan to capture the orphans and get the loot they had "honestly stolen" back. Later than night it was carried out.

"Okay, Will, here is their footprints," Davey replied.

"Yeah, so where are they?" Travis wondered.

"Don't look at me," Johnny said.

"Me either," Will added.

"Let's cross the stream," Johnny suggested, pointing at Sunny Brook, "Maybe they're on the other side."

"And get myself wet?" Davey crossed his arms standing near the deeper edge of the brook.

"Yeah!" Johnny exclaimed pushing on Davey's back causing him to plunge head first into the murky flow of water.

Will pushed Travis' back, who was standing next to Davey. Travis landed right beside Davey with a huge SPLASH!

Davey came up out of the water standing with the water flowing past his waist, "What was that for?"

"Yeah, what did we do?" Travis asked.

"Because you two are both stubborn," Johnny said walking on the stones down the stream from his wet brothers.

"Yeah!" Will added sloshing through the water beside Travis and Davey who had stepped back just in case Will had another trick, like dunking them under.

"We are not," Davey argued, following far behind Will out of the stream.

"Are too, Davey and Travis," Johnny answered looking sternly at Travis, who was slowly walking out the stream behind Davey.

"Come on, ya'll," Will called from a distance almost in an angered way. He had walked up in front of Johnny.

Back at the cave Ash, Jo, and Bo knew that the bandits were on their way, when they had heard the splash and Jo had gone to see what had made it. When she climbed on the top of the cave and had seen Will walking towards her, she went back and told Ash and Bo they were going to have company.

"What will we do?" Ash asked.

"Yeah, Jo, what?" Bo was concerned.

"Uh… go get in a tree that is easy to climb but hard to be seen in, hurry," Jo told them.

Bo went to the pear tree they had gotten their meals out of that day and climbed straight to the top. Ash didn't climb a tree but lay down on top of the cave really still. Jo went behind the cave, after giving Ash a hand up on the cave, and climbed the plum tree near it. They all were still, breathing in slow long breaths. They were quiet, birds chirping, the stream flowing, and brother trying to whisper as they came closer to the kids' cave.

"Orphan kids, where are you?" Will called.

"Oh, kiddie kids, come out, come out," Travis yelled.

"We just want to talk," Davey yelled, then laughed heartedly.

"Yeah, good job, boys," Johnny said sarcastically. "They ought to be out here any minute now."

"Look a cave," Travis pointed ahead.

"Let's go look in it," Will said.

"Okay," Davey said following Will inside the cave. Ash breathed out slowly.

"I'll go look in all the trees," Johnny said starting toward Bo's tree.

Jo was watching Travis when she thought he was going to look up, and then she heard a shout. It was Bo! "Let me go," he screamed. "Jo! Ash! Help!"

"No, little one, now be still," Johnny had got Bo. Jo looked down to see what Travis was doing, as she did, she saw him! Travis had got in her tree silently somehow. Jo started down the other way, between pokey limbs and scratchy leaves, but Travis fought to grab Jo's arm. Ash had gotten up from lying on the cave top. Davey had come out of the cave, but Will was still in there. Ash leaped off the cave and onto Davey's back. They both hit the ground as Jo looked at Ash and yelled.

"No! Ash!" Jo wasn't watching Travis. "Ouch, let me go!"

Travis had grabbed her by the ankles. He had climbed out of the tree, and got right under the limb Jo was on. Travis pulled her to the ground. He fell but got up quickly and picked Jo off the ground. Jo turned her attention back to Ash as Travis took her towards Johnny.

Ash had been nabbed too. He wasn't hurt but Davey now walked with a limp. "You brat," Davey swore.

Travis started discussing what to do now and what Will was doing in the cave still. Jo had thought of a plan really quick, but it wouldn't involve her friends yet. She bit Travis' arm and ran as hard as she could toward the woods the opposite way from the cabin. She ran as Travis swore and Davey took off at a run towards her, letting Ash go. Travis quickly grabbed hold of Ash who started to run too. "Let loose," Ash shouted. "Run Jo! Run Jo, he's oomph," Travis cupped Ash's mouth shut.

"Shush, you vermin," Travis ordered.

"I found the loot," Will said walking out of the cave.

"That's not yours!" Bo yelled.

"It's yours as much as it is ours," Johnny said. "Now shut up! What took you so long?" Johnny looked up at Will.

"They had some other interesting things in there. I put them in this sack with the loot," Will held up a little denim bag.

"That's not yours!" Bo shouted again.

"I said shut up!" Johnny yelled at Bo. Bo lowered his head, because of the loudness that rang through the woods from Johnny's voice.

Jo looked down at Travis who was underneath the tree she had climbed up in to get away from him. Travis walked on, and Jo kept quiet. Travis never showed back up under her tree, but Jo stayed there till midnight just to be safe.

Travis finally wandered back to the cabin, where Davey, Johnny, and Will were discussing what to do with the boys. "Make them our slaves, I tell ya," Will suggested.

"Make them beg for money in the streets," Davey said.

"Yeah!" Travis agreed.

"No," said Johnny firmly. "They are our bait for Jo. She'll come to rescue them, and we'll be ready." He smiled, staring smugly at the tied up boys.

"No," Ash said. Bo shook his head.

"Yeah," the men grinned in unison.

"And keep quiet," Davey ordered.

"Let's put them in my room, till she gets here," Will said.

"I'll help you," Johnny replied, walking over to the chairs, Bo and Ash were tied to.

"Come on, Travis," Davey said pulling on Travis' shoulder, "let's get the guns ready for Jo when she gets here."

Jo climbed down the tall young oak tree she had climbed to get away from Travis. She hurried back to the cave only to find the Bible they had just read the day before strewn all over the rock floor of what she once called home: the black bag of silver and gold was gone. "Everything is gone," Jo said to herself. "Everything but this rope," she grabbed the rope, made a plan in her head, and then ran to the cabin she'd been at before. "God help me save Ash and Bo if it's the last thing I do, besides I owe them."

"Come on in, Johnny. I'll watch out here. You go get some coffee; Travis has been cooking again," Davey stood outside the front door of the cabin, as Johnny stood up and stretched.

"All right," Johnny replied, yawning. "You keep your eyes wide open though."

"I will," Davey said, leaning back in the chair and propping his feet on one of the posts that held up the porch roof.

Johnny went in the house, yelling at Travis, "I told you to count the loot."

"I made you some coffee," Travis pointed at the metal kettle on the pot stove.

"Davey chuckled and closed his eyes, "We need more women folk around here," he smiled, yawning.

Jo watched Davey as he slept, from a tall, young pine tree she had climbed. She tied her rope in a lasso at one and loosely tied the other end to her right wrist. She grabbed a green pinecone from the limb, making the tree shake a little. After assuring herself that the tree was stable again, Jo threw the cone on the porch hitting Davey's foot.

"What in the," Davey leaned up, staring into the woods in front of him. He leaned back, but kept his eyes open on the forest of pine trees. They were thick and hard to tell one tree from the other. Jo threw another green pinecone at the porch, hitting the wall behind Davey's head.

"Who's out there?" Davey stood up quickly, making the chair fall over. Jo threw a third cone at the porch, but it didn't go as far. Only hitting the ground in front of the porch, Davey walked near it, to see if he could tell which direction it had to have come from.

Jo heard Davey's pistols cock. Jo got ready on her limb. Davey walked straight into the woods from the third pinecone Jo had thrown. "Come out, come out wherever you be, little vermin," Davey whispered to a lullaby tune as he walked right under Jo's limb.

Jo let the lasso loop drop around Davey's neck. Before he knew what had happen, Davey was being pulled up from the ground by his shoulders. Not being able to move, Jo made this a good time to throw two more pre-picked large, green pinecones aimed right for the back of his head. The first missed completely, but the second knocked him out cold. Davey's guns dropped to the ground right as all consciousness left him. Jo tied the loose end of the rope from her wrist to the limb near the trunk of the tree. She climbed down, hid the guns from underneath Davey's hung body in a hollowed out log nearby, and snuck to the corner of the front porch. Finally finding a window where she could hear the men talking and watch them, too, she peeked in.

"You grab her," Will told Johnny as he stacked the coins from the loot bag in front of them on the table.

Again, Jo thought sarcastically, smiling. She looked around the room, but saw no sign of Bo or Ash. "Now where are those boys?"

Sneaking around the backside of the cabin, she noticed a window with a bed up against it. "Hmm," Jo wondered. She peaked inside the window and saw them. She tapped lightly on the window, so as not to disturb the men's talking in the other room. Ash's eyes were closed, but Bo looked up. He looked around the room, then seeing Jo, he elbowed the backside of Ash. He hummed loudly, and Jo put her finger to her lips so that Bo would be quieter.

Ash looked up, then Jo saw it. Ash had a bruise under his eye. He had been hit. "Now it's war," Jo promised herself. She tapped softly on the window again. Ash looked her way, and kind of smiled which was hard with a gag on his mouth. Jo gave the same gesture to Ash so that he would be quiet. Ash looked around the room, Jo wasn't sure why. Then she knew, as soon as Ash kicked over the stool beside them. Bo hummed wondering what was done. Ash pushed his feet against the floor making the chair he sat in go up then down with a pound against the floor. Bo had got the idea and so had Jo.

She ducked down under the house, underneath that room, so she could hear what was going on. More things crashed to the floor and more movement of the chair was pounding against the wooden thin floor. Jo thought either the men would get curious and come see what was going on or Ash would jump so much in his chair that they would just fall through the floor. Jo laughed at the thought.

Footsteps and voices started coming from the other room, "What's going on in there?" Will yelled.

Johnny added, "You boys hush. We are trying to think of a plan to kill Jo."

At the word kill, Bo hummed negatively.

Ash still pounded the chair that he was tied to against the floor.

"Go check on them, Travis," ordered Will.

Travis' footsteps got closer to the room that Jo hid under. She listened as Travis came into the room, where Bo and Ash were tied. "What's going on in here? What's the big idea?" Travis looked around the room.

Ash kicked at Travis, hitting the man in his knee. Travis screamed and swore in pain. "Brats!" he yelled. Jo heard a slapping noise.

"No," Jo whispered loudly. "I've got to do something." But then she heard another pair of footsteps coming towards the room.

"What is wrong in here?" Johnny asked.

"Yeah," Will asked from behind Johnny. "What did you do, Travis?"

Travis held his knee, "They kicked me."

"Aww did the kid get kicked?" Will joked. Travis stared angrily at Will, rubbing his knee.

"Stop the commotion, boys or we *will* kill Jo!" Johnny yelled.

Will wandered into the room. "Let's take them in there where we are."

Five pairs of feet shuffled into the den. Gagged humming and slapping sounds were made as Jo crawled under the house and came out under the den window she had been at before.

Jo watched as Ash and Bo were retied back to back in the two three-bar ladder chairs they had been in before. Will and Travis sat down at the table near the window Jo was looking in. She ducked when they walked near her and came up after she was sure they had sat down.

Johnny went onto the front porch. Jo hoped he wouldn't come around the side of the house where she stood. He closed the door mumbling to his self as he sat down at the table with the other two men, causing Jo to duck down again.

"Problem?" Travis inquired Johnny.

"Yeah, Davey decided to take a break on the job," Johnny explained angrily.

"He'll be back soon enough," Will assured Johnny.

"Don't count on it," Jo whispered outside the window, coming back up to look in. She looked at Ash and Bo. Ash had his head down, and Bo was looking up at the ceiling. The trap door lay right on the other side of them. Jo could probably sneak under it and cut her friends free with her boot knife. Jo patted her pockets and then looked at her bare feet. "Or not," she said quietly to herself.

Jo stared through the window at Ash, "Look at me," Jo begged, even though Ash couldn't hear her. He didn't ever look at her. His head was down as if he was asleep. "Must have got slapped again," Jo sighed.

Suddenly Bo looked down from the ceiling and around the room. He spotted Jo at the window; Jo nodded. He elbowed Ash, who looked up, and over behind the bandits at Jo. He shook his head and stared down at the floor once more. Jo looked at Bo, who looked back at Ash. Bo hummed loudly. Ash shook his head once more, to which Bo hummed even louder.

Travis stood up, Jo ducked under the window, "You got something to say, kid?"

He walked in front of Ash, jerking his gag out. "You want to talk?" Ash lowered his head.

"Well?" Will said, sitting at the table. Jo looked back up in the window.

"Nothing," Ash said slowly.

Travis looked back at Johnny, and Jo ducked gasping. "Guess not," Johnny chuckled.

Travis grabbed Ash's jaw and lifted it, "Well?"

Ash looked down blankly. Travis let him go, leaving the gag rag on the floor. He walked over to Bo and jerked the gag out of his mouth, throwing it to the floor, "How about you?"

"Ya'll are all rotten!" Bo screamed. Jo smiled watching Travis rub his ears and swear. Bo kicked at Travis, who dodged grinning.

"Little tough one aren't ya?" he replied.

"Are we now?" Will asked chuckling. "Ash doesn't seem to share your opinion."

"You are all going to jail!" Bo continued.

"Gag him," Johnny ordered. Travis picked the rag back up and tied it back around Bo's mouth. Bo yelled once more nodding at Jo, though Johnny thought Bo was nodding at him, "I can do all things through my Lord Jesus Christ!" Bo tried to bite Travis while he did this, but Travis held Bo's jaw shut, finishing gagging him.

"Shut up," Travis walked back to this chair. Jo slightly ducked, but Travis didn't notice her, so she came back up quickly.

Bo elbowed Ash again; Ash elbowed him back, causing Bo to hum in pain. Ash looked out the window at Jo, who mouthed, "Please?"

Ash nodded, looked at Travis who had started stacking his coins. "Shouldn't you hide your loot before Jo walks in the door and find out what you are doing?"

"Shut up," Travis said angrily. "Jo wouldn't just walk in our door."

"No, the vermin is right. We need to hide this," Johnny replied grabbing the faded denim bag off the table, and sliding his stacked coins into it, he threw the bag into Will's lap, "Put them in."

"Johnny, where are we supposed to hide it?" Travis asked grabbing his stacks, dropping them in the bag as Will held it up. Will tied the bag's looseness in a knot.

Johnny stared at Ash, "Thanks for the idea, kid, but now we have to blindfold you two." Johnny had Travis blindfold Bo.

"No biting, kid," Travis tied his handkerchief around Bo's head tightly. Bo hummed in pain, wriggling his head. Travis grabbed his jaw, "Be still."

Johnny grabbed Will's handkerchief out of his pocket as Will bent down to open the trap door. "Hey!"

"Hey yourself," Johnny yelled back, "I got to blindfold the boy."

"Use yours then," Will said lowering the loot under the house.

"No, mine is for Jo," Johnny said blindfolding Ash.

Will pushed a table over the trapdoor, trying to look natural. The table looked awkward to Jo, it was in between the gun cabinet and the tied up boys.

Jo crawled under the house, quietly picking up the loot and running to the woods with it. Going to the spot where Davey was hung, Jo hid the loot in the hollowed log with Davey's pistols. She ran to the cabin's front door from there.

Out of her pocket, she pulled a piece of paper she had drawn a map of the town on. Jo had drawn an X where she said she would be with the loot. She laid the fake map on the chair Davey had overturned before.

Jo quickly knocked on the door, then hid underneath the house behind the porch steps.

Johnny came to the door, looked both ways out of it, and then saw the map. Jo watched as he walked down the porch, grabbed the map, and listened as he walked back into the house.

"A map!" Travis exclaimed.

"Stupid girl," Will replied. "Thinks she can trade our loot for her boys when our loot is…" Will stopped. "No!" Will ran to the supposedly natural place of the table, pushing it so that it slid into the fireplace.

Ash and Bo elbowed each other in unison, nodded then hummed grumpily at their hurt sides.

"Shut it you two," Johnny said taking the blindfolds off the boys and taking the gag off Bo.

"Bo, she's crazy," Ash whispered.

"Yeah," Bo whispered back.

Will screamed in disbelief, the loot wasn't under the trapdoor.

Travis rubbed his ears, "Whoa, Will, what's wrong?"

"The loot is gone you idiot! Come on, Travis, we are going to get her! Johnny stay with the brats!" Will exclaimed.

"How about Davey?" Travis asked curiously.

"He's coming too! Where is he?"

"He never returned," Johnny replied calmly.

"Fine! Tell him to help you when he returns!" Will said grabbing a rifle out of the gun cabinet and slamming the door behind him before Travis got to the door. Travis opened the door, "We'll be right back with the girl," and closed the door behind him. Will and Travis headed towards town. Jo watched them disappear into the woods. She crawled back underneath the trapdoor.

Johnny sat down at the table, after gagging the boys once more. He played a quick game of solitaire, and then dozed on his crossed arms. Ash stared down at the floor, listening for any sign of Jo. *Surely she didn't go according to the map,* he thought.

Ash looked up startled by a creaking floor sound. Johnny sat up taking his pistol from his gun belt. Then it came again in a creaking, creaking noise. Bo looked around for signs of Jo. "Come on, Jo, I got you covered," Johnny yelled at the front door. Ash watched as a squirrel hopped from the open window in front of him to the wooden floor of the den.

BANG!

"Let that be a lesson to you," Johnny shouted, laying his pistol on the tabletop.

Jo had snuck in the trapdoor, while the squirrel was learning its lesson. Jo quietly opened the gun cabinet near the trap door as Johnny started dozing off again. She took a shotgun just being enough for her to handle, with a little more power of a rifle into her hands and stood up quietly, untying Bo and Ash from the chairs and shushing them.

"Put your hands on your head, Johnny McGuire! And don't even think about grabbing your pistol!" Jo shouted, causing Johnny to leap up off his chair.

"Alright, Jo!" Ash cheered.

"Yeah, stand up, Mister," Bo shouted.

Ash walked over to Johnny, "Not so tough now are ya?"

Johnny grimaced. Bo grabbed his pistol off the table pointing it at Johnny, "Don't move!"

"Yeah, you tell him, Bo," Ash said, grabbing Johnny's knife from his boot. Jo grabbed the rope and the gag rags from the floor.

After Sheriff Nalley had followed the map he received from a demanding carrier pigeon to where Will and Travis, who were wanted for several robberies in cities along the Rainbow River, he continued to follow the instructions in a second note with in the map to get to the little cabin. There he found Johnny and David McGuire tied back to back at the bottom of the pine tree Davey had been swinging in earlier that day. Davey and Johnny, along with their other two brothers were found guilty with kidnapping and theft. They reside in Howling River City Prison for the next thirty years or so.

Jo, Ash, and Bo live in the little cabin in the woods. Ash and Bo were checked by the Sunnyshine town doctor and proven healthy. Jo was checked and found to have a slight allergic reaction to dust. Jo and Ash were given full rights to run the farm on the bandits' land. Bo waits the day that will come when he will be old enough to have full rights with his friends. Until that time, he raises horses for Sheriff Nalley and his deputies. Jo uses her lasso skill to rope strayed cattle for Bo; Ash has planted corn and peas to sell at this year's annual Sunnyshine vegetable fair. The three orphans have settle down in the cabin never to have trouble with bandits ever again.

The End

"I can do all things through Christ who strengthens me."

Philippians 4:13

Printed in the United States
by Baker & Taylor Publisher Services